Published by Archive of the Odd

Formatting and cover design by Cormack Baldwin

Art by Alina Gottbrecht

Content warnings can be found at the back of this book.

ISBN 979-8-9884827-3-4

Lighthouse Logbook No. 28

Daniel Simonson

With Illustration by

Alina Gottbrecht

Lighthouse Logbook No. 28

as transcribed by Merris Edwin Anders

1910 Reunified Era
for the Office of Maritime Records

1681 Shearwater Street, Treppenaire, Khesland

Foreword

“THE SPUR IS NEARLY INVISIBLE once the sun dips low, low beneath the painted sea. A scraggly, jagged vertebrae of stone tracing several miles out from the mainland cape. Most folk have no reason to come here, no rational cause to sail so far north, save for once each year. With the last full moon of spring, as it's just beginning to taste like summer, the crab fishermen venture north. Beyond the Spur, just before the lands narrow again into the Lonesome Strait, the seafloor hosts its most magnificent undersea gala: mating season for the giant moon crabs. Elusive most of the year, preferring to feed on fallen whale carcasses and shipwrecks, the crabs congregate until the moon wanes to quarter once more. The "giant" appellation does not do these crustaceans justice. The oldest and most battle-worn could seat a person atop their carapaces. Fishing for moon crabs is among the most dangerous occupations in the world, to hear old salts and lighthouse keepers tell it. Not because of the crabs. To be sure, they're fearsome and have taken many a fisher's limb. But the waters up north don't take kindly to those who harvest from their bounty, or so folks say. Compasses fail more often than not, and even the stars play tricks with the eye. Oh, the geniuses in learned halls will say it's magnetics or atmospheric distortion. And maybe. Maybe. But the voices over silent waves. Ships piloting alone, hollow shells bereft of crew. Ships with no tangible parts, ghosts in any sense of the word. To say nothing of what oddities breach the waters, favoring lighthouse keepers with a glimpse, before they dive back into their opaque world.

Lighthouse keepers. Now, they're the ones who know as much or more than the fishers. Anything can addle a person's mind at sea, and one knows the reputation sailors have for tall tales. But lighthouse keepers, they meticulously record, and soberly fulfill their assigned duties. After all, if we discount those who keep the lights, who guide us in the dark, who can we trust?"

- From Of the Northern Waters, by Selene Egretta, Master Cartographer at Greater Khes University

I

<u>Day Log:</u> 1st of Meltwater, 1783 Reunified Era

<u>Tide:</u> Low; <u>Weather:</u> Clear

<u>Keeper:</u> Pike

Spied a trawler heading south. No one aboard. Hailed nonetheless. Voice answered back, over water and on comm. Crackled and garbled words on comm, echo too great by ear. No one spotted through the telescope.
The terns are loud today. Excess squabbling, few fish.

<u>Day Log:</u> 3rd of Meltwater, 1783 Reunified Era

<u>Tide:</u> High. Very High; <u>Weather:</u> Miserable.

<u>Keeper:</u> Ellis

Pike says I'm to scribe the next three nights, just for missing one. Judge the fairness of that yourself, whoever reads this. I think I just remind him of his daughter, and he misses having someone to order around. Pike means well, and I caught him almost-smiling yesterday. At terns. Not at me.
Storms have swamped our lonely little spine of rock. Swells echo the thunder above as they crash into the Spur. The terns fled. Pike says this isn't even halfway to the worst storm he's faced. Real storms, he says, make waves like mountains, large enough to swallow the lighthouse itself. The man's been here long enough, I believe it. I'm thankful we've got just a middling storm, elsewise our food stores would be soaked through. Canned mackerel is salty enough without the sea getting involved. Overhead, the light spins round and round, pushing back against the steel clouds. I hope no one is out on the ocean to see it. May all be

home safe from this. But there will be someone. There is always someone sailing these waters, even if their last living journey ended ages ago.

I wonder if I'll stay too, when my watch is over.

Day Log: 4th of Meltwater, 1783 Reunified Era

Tide: Low; **Weather:** Foggy

Keeper: Shale

I'm grateful the storm's passed, but I could do without all this fog. It rolled in right at dawn, when the last thunderclap vanished. The comm crackles every now and then, but no sign of anyone passing by. We couldn't see them anyway, if they did. It had better clear up soon, the mail runner's due sometime today. Rena promised to send photographs of the baby, as often as she can have them taken. I sometimes like to imagine him laughing at the gulls overhead. Or wonder if he'd spit out the pickled plums we ate for breakfast.

Will report when the mail runner makes contact.

Day Log: 4th of Meltwater, 1783 Reunified Era

Tide: Low, rising; **Weather:** Clear

Keeper: Ellis

Second evening on first watch. Lovely and quiet is the night. The fog pressed in all day until sunset, when I suppose the sun decided to get on with it and burn the whole blanket off. Good thing, too. Sitting with that wet clamminess swirling around me all night would be uncomfortable to say the least. Shale's upset, says the mail was due today. I suppose it was, not like I expected anything. Pike says fog can be worse than a storm for navigation, so we ought to be patient with delays. Pike asking anyone to be patient makes me laugh (and yes, you old salt, I know you'll be reading this). No sign of ships now that the sky's clear, either, though.

Dancing lights appeared beneath the waves. Green, blue, red, like spotlights cast from the seafloor. They drifted in lazy circles around one another, then formed up smart as soldiers in a line. Now they've passed in the direction of the Strait, too far out to see at this point. I'll make a note to ask Pike about those in the morning, no one's mentioned lights before.

[Transcriber's Note: Garbled and smudged text]

<u>Day Log:</u> 12th of Meltwater, 1783 Reunified Era

<u>Tide:</u> High; <u>Weather:</u> Overcast

<u>Keeper:</u> Pike

Whales sighted. In water, only. Spouts all through morning, large pod, singing. No whalers on tail. Supply run late, produce stock low. Note: Send Shale and Ellis to gather kelp.

<u>Day Log:</u> 12th of Meltwater, 1783 Reunified Era

<u>Tide:</u> Low, low, low; <u>Weather:</u> Cloudy

<u>Keeper:</u> Ellis

The whales passed by after lunch, but I can still hear the singing. Deep, mournful tones that echo right through to rattle your ribs. Pulsing in your chest. Shale hears it too, keeps shaking his head like a fat old fly is buzzing around. Pike's still up, smoking. Must be in a contemplative mood, that pipe never sees daylight.

We harvested kelp today, Shale and I. Never in my life did I think I'd be boiling seaweed for supper. But the parsnips ran out two days ago, and the cabbage wilted beyond saving. It's a tricky thing, climbing out onto the rocks. Even at low tide, deep pools hide in the gaps between stones. Like miniature oceans themselves, framed with rough walls of mussels. They're not fit to eat, says Pike. Something in the water that's delicious to them but poison to us. Shame, a nice shellfish dinner would go a long way out here. We filled baskets with ropes of knotty kelp. The fronds aren't bad once hot water softens them. Pike eats it raw, straight from the sea. Maybe that's why he's got teeth missing.

Two ships drifted by after midnight. Backwards, and against the current. Neither made contact; not on comm, not with flags. I spied them out with the binoculars, but they're too chipped and fogged up to help much. I don't know if something was dragging those ships along underwater, or if it's some ill omen. I never put stock in omens back home, but you gather superstitions like a child collecting seashells out here.

Whale song must be a good omen, it'll counter anything.

<u>Day Log:</u> 13th of Meltwater, 1783 Reunified Era

<u>Tide:</u> Rising; <u>Weather:</u> Foggy

<u>Keeper:</u> Shale

A quiet morning, with no whales. No whale song. Just this unexpected emptiness they've left behind. We all feel it, even Pike. The sea looks like glass, I've never seen it so calm. Almost as if it's frozen. Frozen and silent.

No ships today, which means no mail either. Fog is to blame again. I hear terns out there, beyond where I can see. I wonder if I can tie a letter to one of them, send it home, let it fly to Rena.

Day Log: 14th of Meltwater, 1783 Reunified Era

Tide: Low; **Weather:** Cloudy

Keeper: Pike

Sky is clearing. Sea still calm, flat and dark. One trawler passed through, little spotlight on it. Hailed and responded, six weeks out of Treppenaire. Shellfish catchers.
A little early, but so it starts.

[Transcriber's Note: A full I5 pages were damaged by water. Only one page legible, fragmentary lines transcribed below - M. E. A.]

...Probably wouldn't want us to....

...Seven of them. Seven! Spewing fumes, ugly things. Rude responses, too...

....When they moved off, Pike made a sign I didn't recognize with his hands. A ward, maybe? My grandfather knew a dozen of those, all banned now. I didn't believe in them when I started here, but with each day...

...Could at least tell us that much.

Weather: Win[dy]

K[eeper]

...Ellis and Pike to make no mention of me [if] we are questioned...

...like static, in my head [...] coming down with something. The tea is awful, but might...

It's doubtless the smoke, blown toward us, from [those] foul...

...crackling, more like a murmur...

Day Log: 29th of Meltwater, 1783 Reunified Era

Tide: Rising; **Weather:** Fair, windy

Keeper: Ellis

In addition to the night watch, I'm supposed to check in on Shale. He's recovering from the voices. Head's still not on straight, but at least he's awake now. Well, not now, at this precise moment. But he's in genuine sleep, not stupor, and for that I'm breathing a little easier. Pike says this oughtn't shake us, it's been known to happen before. But knowing that and feeling it are two different fish. Every time the wind tugs at the lighthouse, I start, ready to plug my ears in case of phantom speakers.

So far, it's just the wind. Just the wind.

A faded-red tin ship pushed through the waters around 0230. They hailed us, and I could hear crackling music in the background of a slightly-inebriated voice over the comms. Crabmen, staking claims before the season starts in earnest. From the Spur down through the quiet harbors back home, the first full spring moon is practically revered. I almost wish I could jump from the tower to that little boat. Join in the music and drink, dreaming of a crab haul worth a king's fortune. I should hail them again, just to hear it.

<u>Day Log:</u> 30th of Meltwater, 1783 Reunified Era

<u>Tide:</u> High; <u>Weather:</u> Storms

<u>Keeper:</u> Pike

First storm of spring. Clouds to the horizon, sky dark as night. Three ships passed and hailed. Advised shelter in cove. Advice ignored. Lightning strikes out on the water. Impact to ships unknown. No further hails. We keep the light.

<u>Day Log:</u> 30th of Meltwater, 1783 Reunified Era

<u>Tide:</u> Unknown, hopefully low; <u>Weather:</u> Storms

<u>Keeper:</u> Ellis

I'm blessed to keep this watch, my grandfather would say. He worshiped in the old way, unification be damned, even now. The Deep Mother and Setting Stars, all of them. Maybe he'll guide a tern or petrel my way to say this storm won't last. He was the only one who wouldn't have sent me off, cast me to the far reaches of civilization. He would've understood.

Ah, sorry Pike. This isn't my diary, I know, I know. But who else is reading this?

Still no sign of, well, anyone through this miserable thrashing. The comms crackle and sputter, but not a word yet. I can't see the ocean to determine the die. Can't even see the jetty to know whether anyone's stranded down there. I hope whoever's on the water, they still see the light.

<u>Day Log:</u> 1st of Stillwind, 1783 Reunified Era

<u>Tide:</u> Low, rising; <u>Weather:</u> Calm, clouds

<u>Keeper:</u> Shale

You would never know the storms shook this place last night. The tide is rising, but slowly. I counted seven ships crossing just this morning. Now, more have arrived. Looks to be a dozen or so sitting out on the water, most have hailed us. A few blessings, a coarse joke. They're in high spirits, with the weather tamed and the crabs arriving.

Would that we had a farther reaching signal. Rena must be worried, our suppliers haven't yet found us. One year, I keep telling myself. One year until everything blows over and I can go home. My father-in-law keeps his word. My son will be too young to remember I left.

<u>Day Log:</u> 1st of Stillwind, 1783 Reunified Era

<u>Tide:</u> High; <u>Weather:</u> Clear and calm

<u>Keeper:</u> Ellis

I've turned the comms up as high as Pike's slumbering will allow. The horizon's a constellation of boats, all hauling up their treasure. They're singing, and shouting orders, breaking open corked bottles. Shale's here too, he's joined in some songs with me, though his voice still cracks like a schoolboy in choir. We haven't got the finest stuff to drink, down in our larders, but it'll have to do. If I close my eyes, I can imagine I'm out there on some heaving deck, lurching this way and that to drag crab traps to the surface.

We heard a fight on board one of the ships, the Aretta, I think. Not between the crew, no, but one crab and six men at least. Someone called for hammers. One man was tossed overboard, and we cheered with rest when they rescued him from the surf. The captain says they're not to eat any catch above a certain weight. Only the littlest ones can the crew keep for free. I wish I could crack open a claw or two with them. To have all that drama, peril, and celebration so close yet out of reach...I'll send Shale for more drinks.

<u>Day Log:</u> 2nd of Stillwind, 1783 Reunified Era

<u>Tide:</u> High; <u>Weather:</u> Cloudy

<u>Keeper:</u> Shale

My head will never be the same. I was content to let Ellis down bottle after bottle of these little stinking brown ales, I was fine with tea, I said, just to keep watch after she'd retired for a few hours. That is, until I had the misfortune to hear the name "Aretta" crackle through the comms. Look, there's lots of Arettas, I'm sure. My grandmother wasn't the only one of her generation. Loads of people name ships after grandmas and wives. But see, the captain had been drinking too, and let slip a few choice words about his employer. Goodness knows I've said the same about my father, but then he mentioned me, and had a second little rant. Damn him, may the crabs take his eyes. I didn't think anyone else knew. I need to get a letter to Rena, quickly.

 Pike, if you've read this far I'm probably already hearing about how I shouldn't use the log for personal matters. I know. But Ellis does it too, and who else shall I talk to? The birds?

<u>Day Log</u>: 3rd of Stillwind, 1783 Reunified Era

<u>Tide</u>: Low; <u>Weather</u>: Clear and windy

<u>Keeper</u>: Ellis

I ought to have guessed I'd get stuck with nights since
Pike set that make-up shift. Not that I mind overmuch,
ships are easier to spot with their lights blinking. As
for the unlit wanderers? Well, I can't record what I
don't see, can I? I wonder how many pass by in the
dark. Moon's not even peering through this tight-knit
blanket of clouds. Fog's starting up, surely because
some great power or another wishes to make my job
harder. I like the clear nights, you'll sometimes see
pale dolphins leaping near shore, when the tide's low.
I've read about them, how something in the blood of
the Spur's herring turns the dolphins' hides a ghostly
silver to cream. I wouldn't mind a bite of herring, even
if it did make me paler than usual. No dolphins tonight,
though. Just a flicker of jellies here and there on the
water, beneath this thickening stew of fog.

<u>Day Log</u>: 3rd of Stillwind, 1783 Reunified Era

<u>Tide</u>: Rising; <u>Weather</u>: Foggy, clearing

<u>Keeper</u>: Pike

Fog moving off. Burning with the sun. Four phantom
hails today. Close, clear, crisp. No ship sighted. Strange
accents. One repeated, dates and time given were
contradictory. Unusual for daylight hours. Jellyfish in
great abundance. Too early, still too early.

II

<u>Day Log:</u> 3rd of Stillwind, 1783 Reunified Era

<u>Tide:</u> Low; <u>Weather:</u> Clear and windy

<u>Keeper:</u> Ellis

A small sailboat's got itself circling out beyond the breakers. There's this little blue-green light atop it, blinking. I've hailed her twice now, no response. Well, not a verbal response, technically speaking. The comms picked up music. First, a downright jaunty dance hall jig, not in any tongue permitted in the Reunified Territories. I wonder what the lyrics meant. No wondering about the second hail, though. A rasping hymn to the Deep Mother, in that strange whisper-singing that's supposed to evoke sighing waves. It's still hissing out of the headset now, which I refuse to wear again until this skiff moves off. Am I meant to report such things, higher up? I won't, obviously. Don't want to answer awkward questions. I can hear it now, "What did you feel, Keeper Ellis? What images popped into your mind?" No, thank you. My own mind's the only thing I have left.

<u>Day Log:</u> 4th of Stillwind, 1783 Reunified Era

<u>Tide:</u> Falling; <u>Weather:</u> Partly cloudy

<u>Keeper:</u> Shale

Praise and curse whatever gods the powers that be will allow! The courier has finally, blessedly, made port. Only now I rather wish he'd delayed. Or lost my mail in particular. No photographs of our sweet boy were in that damp envelope. Instead, my dear wife has apparently noticed the men shuffling in and out of my father's office. She has inquired—inquired!—about my father's fortune. I was promised Rena wouldn't find out. That this would be properly handled. None of it has anything to do with me, I'll set things straight in my next letter. Lucky that captain let his tongue loose the other night, I was able to anticipate some of the damage. But that courier left before the noon bell, leaving me no chance to draft something more specific. Imagine, he has the nerve to say he's on a tight schedule! Well, where was his timeliness weeks ago? I want to go home, to hear my son's name. Would that Rena could write it down, but she keeps to the old superstition. Our son's soul isn't safe until we've each spoken his name to one another. It's not right that I should wait so long, especially for something that isn't technically my fault.

<u>Day Log:</u> 4th of Stillwind, 1783 Reunified Era

<u>Tide:</u> High; <u>Weather:</u> Cloudy and cold

<u>Keeper:</u> Ellis

No family's found me out here, for that I should be thankful. A sight better than Shale, he's more anxious than usual. But I won't pry, wouldn't want to invite him to do the same. Don't worry, Shale, I skipped over your last entry, only read the tide and weather. Your secrets are your own.

That courier brought a meager shipment of food. Mostly tinned. Jarred peaches are a lovely surprise, though. We'd best make them last.

Pike received a ragged book, small and black, with some sort of carving on its wooden cover. I never took him for a reader. He and the courier exchanged a hand signal I didn't recognize from our handbook. Might be religious? I've no clue. Never took Pike for a man of faith, either. Gods don't seem keen to visit this place.

<u>Day Log:</u> 5th of Stillwind, 1783 Reunified Era

<u>Tide:</u> Low; <u>Weather:</u> Rain and wind

<u>Keeper:</u> Pike

Gray dawn, trio of trawlers hailed at noon. First: broken message.Second: Protectorate cant, unintelligible. Third: like-minded captain, shared passages, recitations. They heard whales, two nights prior. Sighted tendrils.

<u>Day Log:</u> 5th of Stillwind, 1783 Reunified Era

<u>Tide:</u> High, falling; <u>Weather:</u> Drizzle drizzle drop

<u>Keeper:</u> Ellis

Nothing feels so lonely as this beacon in the fog and rain. With the sea and sky hidden, you start feeling like the only person in the world. Waiting, watching, staring into the trackless gray.

I wanted to get myself lost, when I left. I've no need to make something of myself, no will to let my life be pushed around like a shuffleboard puck. Pass that marker, achieve those points, make our team look respectable. Let the Ellis name stand tall among the rest. Silliness. I'm an Ellis whether or not I marry some man with more ambition than wit. I'm an Ellis alone, wrapped in fog, spotting ships in the cold, damp dark. Glorious.

<u>Day Log:</u> 6th of Stillwind, 1783 Reunified Era

<u>Tide:</u> Low, rising; <u>Weather:</u> Cloudy, chill

<u>Keeper:</u> Shale

Crab season isn't supposed to be this cold. Even I know that, and in contrast to our senior Keeper, I wasn't practically born on a ship. The crab moon's past, but fishing boats still plough their way through these waters. Four hails today, none mentioning more...clandestine personal matters. For that I am most thankful. If there is any money left when I return home, I'm buying a house far inland. Rena and I will raise our boy far from the trading companies and their calumnious backstabbing. This year cannot pass quickly enough.

A poem of some sort, heavy with static, came through the comms this afternoon. No idea what ship broadcast it, they failed to respond to my questions. Their recitation sounded almost mournful, lines about dark water and forgotten names. Ellis would've liked it, wish I'd written it down for her.

[Transcriber's Note: 10 pages missing, torn out, burnt edges near binding. Logs pick up again without remark]

<u>Day Log</u>: 22nd of Stillwind, 1783 Reunified Era

<u>Tide</u>: Falling; <u>Weather</u>: Sun

<u>Keeper</u>: Shale

Pike says the tide will keep falling until the next full moon. Which apparently happens once every few decades to a century, according to both Pike and the records. Always after the crab moon, and always for precisely one month. All around us, sand flats dry in the sun. It hasn't rained since the crab moon either. Barely a cloud, even. Pike keeps talking about a summer from his childhood, when even the Lonesome Strait was sealed off by a stretch of sandbar. At night, we place a red filter over the light, warning sailors that the sea can't be trusted here. Soon, that won't be enough, the shoreline will be out too far. We'll have to mark the line directly.

<u>Day Log</u>: 23rd of Stillwind, 1783 Reunified Era

<u>Tide</u>: Falling; <u>Weather</u>: Clear

<u>Keeper</u>: Ellis

It's my first night sleeping outside the lighthouse since moving out here. We're camped between a cluster of barnacled rocks, and the wreck of an old fishing boat. Eating canned yams and hardtack. Well, I am, anyway. Pike and Shale decided to try their luck at dreaming. Mine's all spent. Three short hours accompanied by visions of bones. Whales, fish, people. Bones washed into crevices and picked over by slime-oozing hagfish. Then I felt it. The cold, persistent sea. I woke to it filling my bedroll and swaddling me in a salty embrace. Except there was no water. The floor of our tent was the same bed of dry, cracked sand. Shale says I was merely dreaming. But no, I'd woken already by the time I felt it. The ocean was here, in our midst. There's no chance I'll sleep now.

It feels like time is slowing down out here. It's less than ten miles to the sealine, says Pike. Ten miles, we should be there by now. The sand stretches in an endless dark plain. Piles of kelp dry in the sun. Along with fish, dead by the school. We even passed an old whale, crushed under its own weight. The smell is incredible, and not in a good way. Gulls and terns feast on the leavings. Not the whale though, oddly. Even the fish eagles and scrawny foxes give that a wide berth. In the distance, we spied a great three-masted galleon, from those romantic days when the maps had monsters in their blank edges. Pike says not to trust anything we find in it. His superstitions never lead us astray, but I can't help staring at the galleon. A sleeping giant full of stories. It's not far now. I could say I went for a walk. Just a walk, to settle my nerves. No one's coming for us out here anyway, the watch is for...well, I don't quite know. Whichever one of you takes up this log next, I've gone on a little nighttime jaunt.

This is Shale. Same night. Ellis is gone. Ellis is gone and the keening won't stop. Pike went to fetch her, insisted I stay put. That noise isn't inside my head, I know it isn't. This whole tent's shivering with it, and the flies trapped inside with us just dropped from the air, twitching. I keep feeling something trickle out my ears, but they're not bleeding. There's nothing coming out. Nonetheless, cold streaks down my face and there's the keening, that damnable keening.

Stay put. Stay put. Stay put. Stay put. Stay. Stay.

<u>Day Log:</u> 24th of Stillwind, 1783 Reunified Era

<u>Tide:</u> Beyond horizon; <u>Weather:</u> Sun, heat, and more sun

<u>Keeper:</u> Ellis

One shock blanket applied. One cup of bad tea consumed. Enough for Pike to say I ought to report. So yes, here I am, reporting dutiful-like. Not for posterity, not for his records, but for me. I'll spill every last thought like guts on a fishmonger's pier.

The galleon was larger up close. Of course it was, that's how ships and distance work, Ellis. Algae and barnacles covered nearly every spare inch of wood. But for all that, I couldn't find a gap. No, not even a collision break. Like the whole thing sank of its own accord. Thankfully, it fell to its side, the old sleeping behemoth. So I climbed aboard her port side and hoisted myself into the nearest door. Then I lit a match.

That was only my second-stupidest mistake of the evening.

The match barely pushed back the dark, I couldn't see past the first lump of mussels studding the wall below me. Then I saw a leg, armored and pointy and scuttling fast. As large as I am tall. On my honor it was. I dropped the match.

Then every last mussel opened its shell and began making this sorrowful sound. Worse than old ladies singing a dirge. A high-pitched glass-shattering sound, like ringing in your ears. Except it shivered through my whole self, to my bones and teeth. I fell, cutting myself up awfully on the mussels, which were rising and falling like waves. If anything, they started to keen louder, it made my head positively pound. Then I felt the tremble of those scuttling legs again, coming towards me.

The keening reached a pitch I couldn't hear, and then I passed out.

Next thing I remember, Pike was carrying me across the sand, muttering. Not his usual gruff, vaguely annoyed remarks. Saying he had me, I'd be all right. That nothing would hurt me now.

Shale wept when he saw us return. I didn't realize he was so worried.

Day Log: 25th of Stillwind, 1783 Reunified Era

Tide: Falling; **Weather:** Sun

Keeper: Pike

Between we three, carried the wheelbarrow out past the sixth mile. Reminder: Buy a mule next season. Will set up beacons along eighth mile line. Will burn all month.

Note: Do not leave Ellis alone. Not again.

Day Log: 25th of Stillwind, 1783 Reunified Era

Tide: Stagnant; **Weather:** Clear

Keeper: Shale

We made it to the sealine. We're just supposed to traipse on, pretending what happened didn't. I hate how Pike looks at me now. Like I'm made of porcelain, and might shatter any moment. I've half a mind to leap into the ocean and swim for home. But Rena would never forgive me, and I'd never hear our boy laugh. Our boy, how old will he by the time I leave this place? For the rest of my life, I never want to smell or taste the ocean again.

But here we are, at its edge, finally. We arrived early in the morning, and the tide hasn't risen or fallen since. The most demure little waves barely lap against the sand. Pike says the tide's halted, it might sit like this a week or more. So tomorrow we will raise the beacons on stilts and ropes, designed to be doused and drift back to us when the sea returns.

I should hope we arrive before the waves, back at the lighthouse. But a part of me wonders what happens if the sea gets there first.

Day Log: 26th of Stillwind, 1783 Reunified Era

Tide: Rising; **Weather:** Cloudy

Keeper: Pike

Reached lighthouse. Tide returned, full force. Small fishing boat wrecked on rocks, just prior to sunset, investigating presently. Neither ships nor seabirds sighted.

Day Log: 26th of Stillwind, 1783 Reunified Era

Tide: High; **Weather:** Cloudy

Keeper: Ellis

Now, I know you're not leaving off like that, Pike. "Reached lighthouse. Tide returned." Grandest understatement of the decade, I bet you. Here's what happened: After striking camp at dawn, we made it within view of the lighthouse by midday. The sun was out, the whole plain stank of rotted fish and I swear I swallowed half a dozen flies. About an hour later, there came a sound, like thunder far-off. We looked back. We shouldn't have, oughtn't have given it a moment's thought and just pressed on, but we looked back. The ocean was coming full-force. It took days for the tide to fall, and only one afternoon to rush in again. Pike says he's never seen anything like it since his first year here (however long ago that was). So no, we did not just "reach the lighthouse," we scrambled up the rocks in full panic and left our tent and sleeping bags to the water's mercy.

And about that wreck: the little fishing trawler coughed up by the tide had no one aboard. Half-stocked provisions, so there's some luck on our end. No sign of what happened to her original crew. We'll salvage what we can. The tide's done rising for now, and with dawn approaching, hasn't fallen an inch near as I can tell. Still, quiet, as if it didn't try to consume us today.

<u>Day Log:</u> 27th of Stillwind, 1783 Reunified Era

<u>Tide:</u> Rising; <u>Weather:</u> Fair

<u>Keeper:</u> Shale

For months, I yearned to be free of this place, now I can hardly step out the door without shaking. That horrendous wall of water rushes over me every time I close my eyes. Had we been a few heartbeats too late, the sea would have dragged us out, never to touch dry land again.

That's not what frightens me, though. Not what sets my teeth chattering. No, it's the gut-deep want eating away at my insides. For the sea to return. For white foam to cover me and fill my nostrils. I know it makes zero rational sense, this longing, I know it was alien to me before we set out on that accursed little camping trip. I hate it. But my thoughts linger over the taste of saltwater and the freedom of floating, floating, floating.

No. I will return to Rena. To Rena and our son,

whose name I will hold and echo to her.

Right. Business. Business. No ships to report, nothing of note in the water save jellyfish, more than I've ever wanted to see at once. I need to leave this lighthouse, before I cannot.

<u>Day Log</u>: 27th of Stillwind, 1783 Reunified Era

<u>Tide</u>: Low; <u>Weather</u>: Clear and cloudless

<u>Keeper</u>: Ellis

Jellyfish. Unfathomable numbers of jellyfish, squelching over the rocks, mingling in the waters all day. Already the air stinks with the ones the sea discarded. Shale and I ventured down sometime around dinner, and that was a pretty mistake, let me tell you. Nothing turns the stomach like that smell. And the sight of them, most so heavily degraded they're like waterlogged rags or globs of what you'd sneeze out. But the intact ones were the most difficult to look at. No mistaking the patterns of deep red dots and lines over their button-smooth tops. Faces. Stretched and distorted, but blank, almost serene. Shale says it's some sort of "pareidolia," which he explained as if I'd never picked up a book in my life. I went to University, I told him, a real one, too. I know what pareidolia is. But these faces, if you sort of look at them from the side, start taking on depth and detail. No little quirk of evolution would etch that into a faceless, practically mindless, bag of water and tissue. Whatever these jellies are, I want no part of them.

<u>Day Log</u>: 28th of Stillwind, 1783 Reunified Era

<u>Tide</u>: High; <u>Weather</u>: Cloudy, fog

<u>Keeper</u>: Pike

Fog will not relent. Terns heard but not seen. No hails on comms. Potential ship spotted. Incongruous and unlikely. Three masted, by its outline. It cannot be. It must not be. Yet it is.

<u>Day Log:</u> 28th of Stillwind, 1783 Reunified Era

<u>Tide:</u> Low, rising; <u>Weather:</u> Clear

<u>Keeper:</u> Ellis

I don't want to record what I've seen. It should not be etched in ink for the world to see, for anyone to remember. Had I been alone, I'd assume my mind decided to toss reality out the highest window. But Pike witnessed it, as did Shale.

The fog pressed in against the windows as we ate dinner, before my watch began. Perhaps we might have seen it, otherwise. Through the wind, Shale said he heard shouting. Now, Shale's ears are happy to invent sounds of their own accord, lately. But Pike sat up stiff as a week-old corpse and listened. Pike's face is dour more often than not, but that was the first time I'd ever seen him truly sad, practically mournful. He told us to "ignore them." Why he thought I'd ever do that, I can't imagine. So I ran up those stairs, to the light, to our never-failing beacon. Then I saw it.

A ship, three-masted and in full sail, lurching toward us over the waves. An impossible ship, translucent like the fog. I saw the white caps through its hull. But fog doesn't shout, doesn't cry out in terror and beseech forbidden gods. It sped on, dead set for the rocks below. Then a horrendous crash, like the world breaking open, and wailing that's still echoing in my head. Some of the men - translucent as their boat, struck the rocks and lay there for a moment, before evaporating into the fog. Others bobbed in the water like so many forsaken corks. Then their screams turned to something more rhythmic. Their bodies lined up smart as festival swimmers. And they, too, were gone. So was the fog. Pike reached the top of the lighthouse then, staring out at the vanishing shapes in the fresh moonlight. Told me their prayer was answered, they were heard, and I should think no more of it.

But that scene plays over and over if I close my eyes. The screams, the splintering boat, and the sudden change in those men's voices. All chanting as one, all fear gone. Who were they? And why did I see this?

Day Log: 29th of Stillwind, 1783 Reunified Era

Tide: High, falling; **Weather:** Half-light

Keeper: Pike

Sun caught midway in rising. Will not set. It is happening again. I hear you now, even now.

Day Log: 29th of Stillwind, 1783 Reunified Era

Tide: Low, too low; **Weather:** Impossible

Keeper: Shale

I don't care that Pike has already logged the day. That isn't enough, isn't nearly enough, for what we're enduring right now. I feel the swell of the surf in my chest, like the whole sea has seeped into me and is pulling, pushing, pulling, pushing. My feet won't carry me but a few steps. And the...I want to call it humming, but that doesn't do it justice. Almost like music, or the static that is even now leaking from the comms system. Why is it always me who hears the strange things? But it's not only me this time, Pike is listening. Ellis, too. Perhaps they're hiding it better but they do not look scared. Then again, I don't believe I've ever seen Pike afraid of anything.

The sea will have me. I am sure of this now. So, Rena, tell our son's name to the world in my absence. And know that I am sorry, genuinely, heart-wrenchingly sorry for my part in my father's schemes. I pretended not to know where the money came from. I looked the other way as he paid off port officials to confiscate rivals' shipments. Scuttled local fishermen's crews. Oh, Rena I am a coward first and foremost, and you deserve to know this. If the courts aren't too corrupt now, our name will be tarnished from Treppenaire to Galfist to the Setting Stars islands for all I know. But you've a right to know, a right to free yourself from the weight that will drown me. You may give my name back at the courthouse, if you wish. Yours was the better anyway.

I am sorry, and I love you, until the sea covers all.

<u>Day Log:</u> 29th of Stillwind, 1783 Reunified Era

<u>Tide:</u> Rising fast; <u>Weather:</u> Sunrise? Set?

<u>Keeper:</u> Ellis

I'm not sure if there's a point in calling this a night log anymore. Night, day, they've had no meaning since what ought've been dawn this morning. But the sun is caught at the horizon, as if an anchor holds it down. Stars still burn overhead, and there's this sound, the same rhythm as that keening I heard in the overturned ship on the tidal flats. Shale's beside himself, quite literally. He's mumbling to himself, curled up on the floor. Another Shale sits mirrored beside him every so often, backs turned to each other, at the pauses in the thrum. Pike hasn't slept in...Deep Mother knows how long.

No ships have hailed, nor do I think they could, our comms are full of static echoing the vibration around us. No ships on the horizon, but the water isn't empty either. Tendrils flashing with lines of colored light, like lightning in reds and blues and yellows. Ribbons of color arcing through the water, with blooms of concentric rings splitting off from them. No, not rings. I see them now, in the half-light on the eastern side. Jellyfish. Tens of thousands, millions maybe, sprouting from tendrils laying just below the surface of the sea. The water is still, so still it seems almost to not be there. As if the jellyfish and their gargantuan source are floating in a dark empty void just off the rocks. The thrumming has a new key now. It's...beautiful. There is no other word for it. Would that this song could last forever. Forever.

Shale is getting to his feet. Pike too. But he

Day Log: Day or Night Irrelevant. 30th of Stillwind, 1783 Reunified Era

Tide: High, rising; **Weather:** Sonorous

Keeper: Pike

Let it be recorded. Let it be known. I came to this Spur Lighthouse from the merchant ship Abalone at fourteen years of age. Following the ghost ship Sendra's Mercy sighted ten days prior. Following so closely we met the same fate that she had, nigh on two centuries prior. But the men I served under did not die. Not a one of them drowned off this shore. The water filled with song and color. Jellyfish by the millions, and arms stretching for leagues unmeasured. Each man joined to an outstretched arm, going clear

and soft and strange. One by one, save me. I was
bouyed by a raft of jellyfish with men's faces, carried
to the rocks, and discarded.

This was no god known to the Reunified world. I'm
certain of this, it was not the Deep Mother, but
something more primal. Something that left me here,
to wait. Not to hope, just wait. To wait, even when I fled
the lighthouse and sought an ordinary man's life. To
wait, until this beacon called me back again.

And now, my waiting has ended.

Day Log: 10th of Amberlight, 1783 Reunified Era

Tide: Low; **Weather:** Partly sunny

Keeper: Ellis

Ten days. Ten days I lay with that thrumming pulsing
through every bone, barely able to eat or sleep. Ten
days since Shale and Pike gave themselves to the
seething, ancient thing that filled our desolate bay. The
entity that sings forever and can never die, renewing
itself, always.

But it left me. It left me, and there's this hollow
space in my mind and my chest that echoes every time
I move.

I came to this splinter of rock to disappear. Fully
and utterly, never to be found by those who knew me.
By those who wanted only the person they'd convinced
themselves to see. And now? Perfect, complete
disappearance danced right in front of me, in radiant
rainbows. Disappearance. Dissolution. Recombination.
That's what it sang of, what it always sings of.

It took Shale, first. The poor man was barely
conscious as the sea battered open the doors below.
Shale, himself and his bizarre reflection-self, stood and

sort of shambled toward the stairwell. He hummed a tune we all recognized by then, and slipped over the railing of the spiral stairs. We did not hear him hit the bottom. Should I have stopped him? Perhaps. But what could I have done? The tide rose higher and higher. If Pike hadn't leapt from the gallery, the waves might have toppled the entire lighthouse. He plunged into the surf with the first true smile I think I'd seen on his face. Missing teeth and all.

Now, there's only me. Ten days later. The Maritime Services Corps sent word that two new recruits will be sped along to me soon. As the most senior Keeper here, I'm to show them the ropes, as it were. And here I'll wait, until that echoing hollow spot is filled with song.

Two ships hailed this morning, sending up shanties my grandfather knew. The sky is clear and blue, and the terns have come to nest again.

Content Warnings

Isolation, deteriorating mental state, death

About the Author

Daniel Simonson is an elementary school teacher in Pennsylvania, who also trains students in the art of dice-rolling tabletop games. He frequents libraries and out-of-the-way bookstores often enough that strange books do turn up, from times and places forgotten. Daniel's siblings advised him to have less books, but instead he obtained more shelves. It's entirely possible that contained in those shelves was Lighthouse Logbook No. 28, but he's required to say that is mostly speculation.